- A veterinarian appointment for a checkup and shots
- Cat litter and a litter box
- Quality food for your kitten or cat
- Special cat treats
- Ceramic or stainless-steel food and water dishes (no plastic)
- A cat brush or comb
- Safe toys that cannot be swallowed
- A scratching post or other cat furniture
- A safe indoor home, especially for kittens

zzzz

Our New Kittens

by Theo Heras

Illustrations by Alice Carter

pajamapress

Two tiny kittens,
brothers,
just like us.
We have been waiting for weeks.
Now they are big enough to
come home.

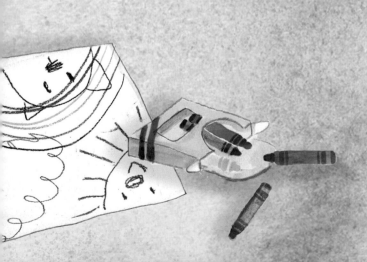

"What will we call our kittens?"
my little brother asks
as we take them gently into our laps.

We want to hold them in the car,
but the cat carrier is safer.
Two tiny kittens mew as we
drive home.

In our room, we open the carrier.
One kitten runs out to explore.
The other hides inside.

I call it softly and wait.
The kitten peeks out, curious,
sniffing the new smells of his
new home.

My brother chases the first kitten.
It hides under the bed.

"Kittens don't like to be chased," I say.
My brother stops.
"What will we call our kittens?" he asks.

The kitten reappears.
It climbs into my brother's lap.
Two tiny kittens fast asleep.

Just like that, they are awake
and ready to explore again.
First, we show them
the kitty litter box.

They sit in it and scratch.
WHAT A MESS!
Out they scramble.

Next, we show them their food and water bowls.
They sniff and try the kitten food.
They lap the water.

Off they go.
More exploring!

We have two of everything:

Two water bowls,

Two food bowls,

Two litter boxes.

Two tiny kittens,
One kitty bed to share.
Two sleepy heads.

Awake again!
Two little balls of fur tumble as they run.
My brother jumps and shouts for joy...
and the kittens hide under the chair.
"Too noisy! Let's whisper."
We sit and make soft sounds.
"What will we call our kittens?"

Soon the kittens return.
They rub their heads against our knees.
You belong to me, they seem to say.
We scratch behind their ears and
brush their coats.
"I hope you like your new home," I say.
"We'll have so much fun," whispers
my brother.

Boots and Scruffy,
two tiny kittens,
brothers,
just like us,
purr and purr.

First published in Canada and the United States in 2018

Text copyright © 2018 Theo Heras
Illustration copyright © 2018 Alice Carter
This edition copyright © 2018 Pajama Press Inc.

This is a first edition.

10 9 8 7 6 5 4 3 2 1

www.pajamapress.ca   info©pajamapress.ca

Canada Council   Conseil des arts
for the Arts   du Canada

ONTARIO ARTS COUNCIL
CONSEIL DES ARTS DE L'ONTARIO
an Ontario government agency
un organisme du gouvernement de l'Ontario

Canadä

The publisher gratefully acknowledges the support of the Canada Council for the Arts and the Ontario Arts Council for its publishing program. We acknowledge the financial support of the Government of Canada through the Canada Book Fund (CBF) for our publishing activities.

Library and Archives Canada Cataloguing in Publication

Heras, Theo, author
Our new kittens / by Theo Heras ; illustrations by Alice
Carter. -- First edition.
ISBN 978-1-77278-060-4 (hardcover)
I. Carter, Alice, 1977-, illustrator II. Title.
PS8615.E687O87 2018   jC813'.6   C2018-901767-8

Publisher Cataloging-in-Publication Data (U.S.)

Names: Heras, Theo, 1948-, author. × Carter, Alice, 1977-, illustrator.
Title: Our New Kittens / by Theo Heras ; illustrations by Alice Carter.
Description: Toronto, Ontario Canada : Pajama Press, 2018. × Summary: "Two young brothers care for their new kittens. The younger wonders what they will name their new pets while his older brother teaches him to be quiet and gentle while they introduce them to food and water dishes, litter boxes, a bed, and grooming brushes"— Provided by publisher.
Identifiers: ISBN 978-1-77278-060-4 (hardcover)
Subjects: LCSH: Brothers – Juvenile fiction. × Kittens – Juvenile fiction. × Pets – Juvenile fiction. × BISAC: JUVENILE FICTION / Animals / Cats. × JUVENILE FICTION / Family / Siblings. × JUVENILE FICTION / Social Themes / New Experience.
Classification: LCC PZ7.H473Ou ×DDC IEI – dc23

Original art created with colored pencil, watercolor and digital
Cover and book design by Rebecca Bender

Manufactured by Qualibre Inc./Print Plus
Printed in China

Pajama Press Inc.
181 Carlaw Ave. Suite 251 Toronto, Ontario Canada, M4M 2S1

Distributed in Canada by UTP Distribution
5201 Dufferin Street Toronto, Ontario Canada, M3H 5T8

Distributed in the U.S. by Ingram Publisher Services
1 Ingram Blvd. La Vergne, TN 37086, USA

In memory of Corky and Falkor
—T.H.

For my wonderfully supportive
family, and Puff and Pepper,
the coolest cats I know
—A.C.

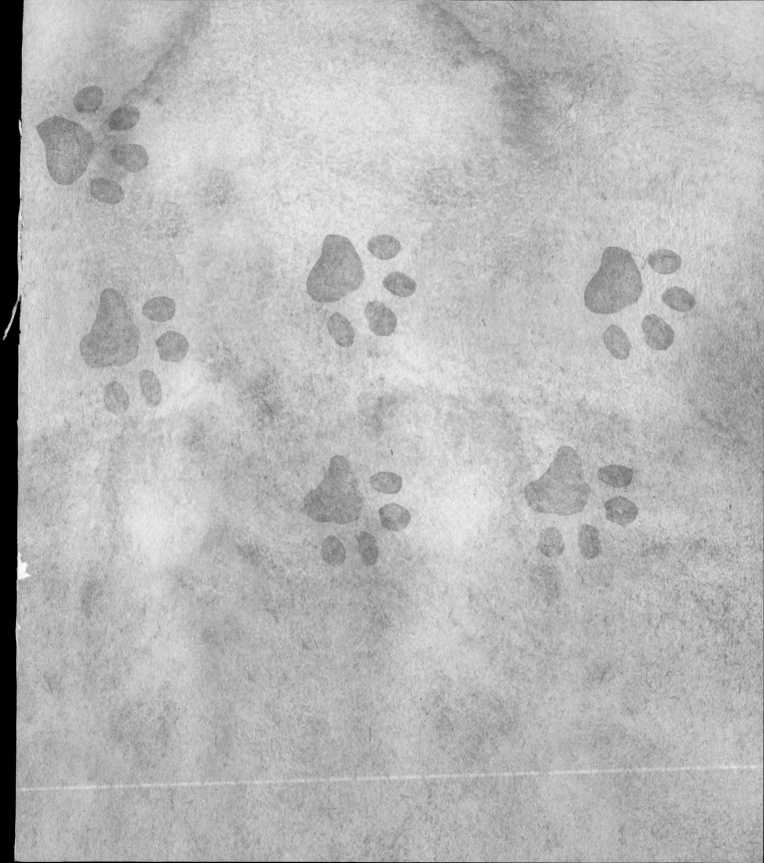

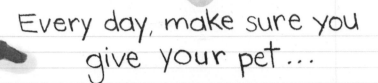

Every day, make sure you
give your pet...

- Fresh water
- Fresh food
- A clean litter box
- Clean floors
- A good brushing
- Playtime and lots of love!